OH
BROTHER

OH BROTHER

SONYA SPREEN BATES

ORCA BOOK PUBLISHERS

Library and Archives Canada Cataloguing in Publication

Title: Oh brother / Sonya Spreen Bates.
Names: Bates, Sonya Spreen, 1963– author.
Series: Orca currents.
Description: Series statement: Orca currents

Identifiers: Canadiana (print) 20190168897 | Canadiana (ebook) 20190168900 |
ISBN 9781459824331 (softcover) | ISBN 9781459824348 (PDF) |
ISBN 9781459824355 (EPUB)

Classification: LCC PS8603.A8486 043 2020 | DDC jc813/.6—dc23

Library of Congress Control Number: 2019947365
Simultaneously published in Canada and the United States in 2020

Summary: In this high-interest novel for middle readers, Lauren is worried about
what will happen when her new friends realize her brother is disabled.

*Orca Book Publishers is committed to reducing the consumption of
nonrenewable resources in the making of our books. We make
every effort to use materials that support a sustainable future.*

Orca Book Publishers gratefully acknowledges the support for its publishing
programs provided by the following agencies: the Government of Canada,
the Canada Council for the Arts and the Province of British Columbia
through the BC Arts Council and the Book Publishing Tax Credit.

Edited by Tanya Trafford
Cover artwork by gettyimages.ca/darenwoodward
Author photo by Megan Bates

ORCA BOOK PUBLISHERS
orcabook.com

Printed and bound in Canada.

23 22 21 20 • 4 3 2 1

For Katie and Emily

Chapter One

Lauren stared out the window of her new room at the street below. It seemed a long way down. She was only one floor up, but it seemed more like three. She picked at a bit of flaking paint on the windowsill and watched as it spiraled through the air toward the ground. Out on the street the moving van was parked half in and half out of the driveway, boxes and furniture stacked floor to ceiling. Two men were trying to slide her mom's baby grand piano out of the truck.

Lauren sighed. She felt all funny inside. Empty and hollow, with little butterflies fluttering around. They'd only left Ash Creek the day before, but she missed her friends already. Her hand went to the locket hanging around her neck, closing it in her fist and giving it a squeeze.

"So we can always hang out together," Kat had said when Lauren opened it and saw the picture from their camping trip the previous summer. She'd laughed as she said it, but they'd been best friends for years, and Lauren could tell that Kat was just as sad as Lauren was.

"Lauren?" Her mother's faint voice drifted up through the floor.

"Yeah, Mom?"

"Come down here, please."

Her mom was in the dining room, where the piano was now. She sat on the piano stool, her back to Lauren, running her hands along the keys. Lauren was reminded of the days when her mom used to spend hours and hours practicing, the music flowing from her fingers.

"There you are," said her mom, standing up briskly. "The movers will be unloading for another couple of hours at least. Why don't you take Will down to the park?"

Lauren rolled her eyes. "Aw, Mom. I wanted to get my room set up."

"You can do that this afternoon." She patted Lauren's arm. "It'll do you both good. He's in his room with your dad."

Lauren frowned as her mother raced off after the movers again. All she'd talked about lately was the move. How Vancouver was close to everything, which meant no more long drives to appointments or hospitals. How great the new school was and the amazing programs they had for Will. No one had given a thought to what it would mean for Lauren, let alone asked her how she felt about it.

Will's eyes lit up when he saw his sister. Lauren couldn't help grinning back at him.

"Hey, Will," she said. "Want to go to the park?"

Will's smile got bigger, and he waved his arms around excitedly.

Lauren's dad looked up from where he kneeled on the floor, screwing the railing onto Will's bed. "That sounds like a great idea. Why don't you take him past the school on your way? That way it won't be so unfamiliar on Monday."

Lauren watched as her dad put Will's jacket on, then lifted him off the floor and set him gently in his chair.

"Make sure you put the brake on if you stop on a hill," he said, tightening the straps that kept Will sitting upright.

"Yeah yeah. I know the drill," said Lauren.

She grasped the handles of the wheelchair and headed out.

"So, Will, where to first? School or park?" she asked once they got outside.

"School!" said Will, pointing and nodding his head.

Lauren turned left and began pushing the wheelchair up the steep slope, grunting with the effort. She didn't stop until she reached the top.

There it was. Birch Park Elementary. Her new school, and Will's as well. Just thinking about it made her stomach tie itself into a knot.

They'd had a tour before Christmas, to meet the principal, enrol in classes and discuss Will's special needs. The place was a maze of hallways. She would have got totally lost if her dad hadn't been there. Classrooms, gymnasium, library, multipurpose room, more classrooms.

"You sure you want to go down there?" she asked Will.

Will nodded.

"Can't it wait until Monday?"

Will shook his head no.

Lauren sighed. "All right." Then she grinned. "Do you want to race?"

Will squealed and waved his arms.

"Ready, set, GO!"

Lauren gave the chair a big push to get it rolling. Then she sneaked up beside it as it barrelled down the hill. She kept one hand on the push handle to keep the chair going straight. The front wheels rattled. Will laughed, his mouth wide open in delight. He pounded his hand on the armrest.

"You won't beat me!" Lauren shouted. She ran faster, pulling ahead.

Will laughed even harder.

They were almost at the bottom of the hill, the school only a few feet away, when someone stepped through the school gate.

"Look out!" Lauren shouted.

She grabbed Will's chair, her sneakers skidding on the gravel beside the sidewalk. The chair tipped onto two wheels, then thumped back down as Lauren dragged it to a stop.

She stood there, panting and gasping for air, and looked up to see the face of her new school principal.

Chapter Two

"Hello, Mr. Burman," Lauren said.

"Lauren Scanlon." The principal's bushy eyebrows sat like a straight line on top of his glasses. "Perhaps you can explain to me what you were doing just now?"

"I—we—" She looked at Will. "We were just having fun. Will likes to race."

Mr. Burman's face turned a shade darker. "Do you know how dangerous that is? You could have seriously injured him. He's not like other children, you know."

Something tightened around Lauren's heart. Of course she knew that. It wasn't Mr. Burman who had lived with Will for the last six years. Lauren was the one who helped feed him and dress him and push him around the supermarket or to the playground. She was the one who hardly ever had any time with her mom and dad because they were always busy with Will. She was the one who was now facing life in a strange school so that her brother could get the help that wasn't available in Ash Creek.

"I would never do anything to hurt him," she said. "He's my brother."

Mr. Burman's brows relaxed. "No, of course you wouldn't, not intentionally.

But you need to take care with him. He's special."

"Yes, Mr. Burman," Lauren said. She waited for him to walk to his car and drive away before she pushed Will's chair through the gate.

The school grounds were eerily quiet. Lauren and Will went slowly around the buildings, sticking to the concrete path so Will's chair wouldn't get stuck in the soft, wet grass. In two days Lauren would be back here. The yard would be teeming with kids, and she would be facing a new class of sixth and seventh graders, knowing no one, starting in the middle of the year.

Standing on tiptoe, she peeked through a window into one of the classrooms. It was dark inside, but she could make out a few large tables, chairs stacked next to them, rows of bag hooks, artwork hanging from the ceiling, posters on the wall, a couple of computers. Her stomach tightened even more.

"Swing!" said Will.

Lauren looked a minute longer, then grabbed the handles of his chair. "Not here," she said. "Let's go to the park."

The park was almost as quiet as the school had been. The only people around were a few kids playing soccer and a gray-haired woman in a tracksuit throwing a ball for her dog.

Lauren strapped Will into the toddler swing and gave him a push, then hopped on the other swing.

"More," Will said.

"I'm not pushing you any higher," said Lauren. "You've got me in enough trouble already."

"More!"

"No."

Lauren turned away from her brother and stared across the field. A black cloud was fogging up her brain. Why

11

couldn't they have stayed in Ash Creek? Her friends were there, and her gran and Aunt Sofie. Everyone had said she was the best dancer in her dance class, and her piano teacher, Mrs. Walsh, had let her play jazz and funk even though her mother really wanted her to play classical. And no one had taken any special notice of her and Will. No one had bossed her around or told her to be careful, not to push him too high on the swing or go too fast with the chair.

The sound of shouting drifted her way, and Lauren turned her attention to the soccer game. There were six kids, playing three-on-three. Five boys of various sizes and a girl with a cap on backward. Did they go to her school?

She watched as the girl chased after the ball, her legs flying. A small boy with blond hair reached it first and kicked it toward the goal. The girl dived for it, and the ball shot away.

"Saved!" she cried. She jumped up, her cap now on the ground, mud on her shirt, and her long hair falling in her face.

The ball came to rest a few feet from Lauren. She stared at it for a moment and then went to pick it up.

"Thanks," said one of the boys, running toward her. He held up his hands for her to throw it to him, and his eyes drifted over her shoulder to Will. His smile faded.

Lauren threw the ball hard, and it thumped into his hands. Then she sighed as he ran back to his friends without another word.

"Let's go home," she said.

Chapter Three

Monday morning dawned bright and sunny, but Lauren still felt as if a thundercloud was hanging over her head. Dragging her feet, she trudged downstairs to the kitchen.

Will was obviously excited. Lauren sat next to him, but the thought of eating anything made her feel sick. She took a sip of orange juice and made a face.

"Stop wriggling before you knock something over," she snapped as Will flailed his arm wildly over his breakfast.

His smile drooped, and she immediately felt guilty for yelling at him. Frowning, she shoved her chair back from the table.

"Lauren, you haven't eaten anything," called her mom.

"I'm not hungry," she said and went to brush her teeth.

In the bathroom she stared at herself. "Stop being such a wuss," she said to her reflection. "It's just school. They're just kids. Get over it."

Their mom drove them to school. It was still early, so there were only a few kids in the yard. They got Will's wheelchair out of the car and made their way to the office. Mr. Burman was working at his desk, but he rose and held out his hand to Lauren's mom when he saw them.

"Mrs. Scanlon," he said. "So good to see you again." He smiled at Lauren. "Hello, Lauren. Ready for your first day?"

Lauren nodded.

"Lo!" said Will.

Mr. Burman glanced at Will but didn't reply. He turned his attention back to Lauren's mom.

"We've got everything ready for Will," he said. "I asked Ms. Westhaven to come in a bit early so we could get him settled. I'll show you the way."

Lauren looked down at Will. His grin had disappeared. She gave his hand a squeeze. "Don't mind him," she whispered as she wheeled him out the door. "He's just an old grouch. I'm sure your teacher is really nice."

They followed Mr. Burman through the hallways. Kids were starting to arrive, and curious eyes followed them as they passed. It made Lauren's stomach churn even more than it already was. She was glad she hadn't eaten any breakfast.

Finally they arrived at Will's classroom. They were greeted by a young woman who smiled at them all and then crouched down in front of Will's chair.

"You must be Will," she said, taking his hand. "I'm Ms. Westhaven, your new teacher. I'm very happy to have you in my class."

Will grinned his biggest grin of the day. "Lo!" he said.

"As we discussed, Will's educational assistant, Miss Chatwal, will be here at nine thirty," Mr. Burman said to Lauren's mom. "I'm sure Ms. Westhaven can manage until then."

With a brisk nod of his head, he left. Lauren's mom showed Will's teacher his communication board and began explaining his feeding routine. Lauren looked out into the hall. It was filled with kids now, talking and laughing. A few little kids came into the class and started putting away their jackets and schoolbags. They all stared at Will.

"Mom," Lauren said. She tapped her mother on the arm. "I have to get to class. I think the bell's about to ring."

"Oh yes, of course, Lauren, you go on. I'll be a few more minutes here." Her mom gave her a quick hug. "Have a good day."

"But—I don't know where my class is," said Lauren. She could feel tears pricking at the back of her eyes and quickly blinked them away.

"Whose class are you in?" asked Ms. Westhaven.

"Mr. Pittman's."

"Just go up the stairs at the end of this hall to the second floor. He's in room 215, on the left, a few doors down." She smiled and turned her attention back to Will.

"Room 215. Second floor," she said to herself as she stepped out into the hall.

She looked to the left and saw an EXIT sign at the end of the hall and a bunch of kids disappearing around the corner. She took a deep breath and plunged into the crowd.

She followed the flow of kids to the stairs. When she got to the top, she tried to get a glimpse of the room numbers as she was swept along…201…205… By the time the crowd had thinned enough to spot a number again, she was at room 225. She'd missed it.

She heard the final bell ring, and her heart gave a thump of panic. It was her first day, she was late already, and she still didn't know where she was going. This was her worst nightmare coming true.

Suddenly a girl came racing out of the stairwell at the other end of the hallway. She was going so fast she almost ran into Lauren.

"Whoa! Sorry," she cried.

Lauren blinked at her. It was the girl from the park.

"Hey, you okay?" the girl said.

"Yeah—I mean, not really. It's my first day and I'm—I'm kind of lost." Lauren's lip trembled, and she bit down on it.

The girl tilted her head. "Don't worry about it. Whose class are you in?"

"Mr. Pittman's. Room 215."

"That's my class. Cool. C'mon." She started walking down the hall. Lauren followed. "I'm Callie, by the way."

"Lauren."

"You just move here?"

Lauren nodded. She opened her mouth to say more, but Callie put a finger to her lips as they reached room 215.

"This is our classroom," she whispered. "Mr. Pittman hates it when kids are late. Says it shows disrespect.

Of course, it's only your first day, so he probably won't go too hard on you, but me…" She rolled her eyes.

The whole class looked up as they walked in.

"Callie Walker, you're late."

Mr. Pittman looked a bit scary.

"I hope you have a valid excuse," he said to Callie. His frown disappeared when he saw Lauren.

"You must be Lauren." He looked at a paper on his desk. "Lauren Scanlon?"

"Yes," said Lauren. "I'm sorry we're late. I got kind of lost, and Callie helped me find the classroom."

Mr. Pittman smiled at her. "Well, thank you, Callie," he said. "And welcome, Lauren. Now go find a seat."

Callie had already plunked herself down at a table at the back with three other girls. She grinned at Lauren and mouthed thanks.

Lauren found a spot near the front,

across from a boy with a long ponytail. He stared at her for a minute but didn't say anything. Lauren took a deep breath. She'd be okay. It was only the first day. Things would get better.

Chapter Four

Math, spelling, French. The school day already seemed like it had lasted for days instead of hours. The boy with the ponytail, whose name was Byron McAfee, continued to stare at her, but, despite her attempts to be friendly, didn't utter a word. The other two kids at her group of desks were twins, a girl and a boy, who introduced themselves as Alicia and Alex. They worked quietly with their heads bent and their matching curly dark hair falling into their faces.

Lauren peeked over at the other tables. Some kids were talking quietly as they worked. Others seemed to have finished. Callie and two of the other girls were laughing behind their books. It didn't look like they were getting much work done.

Mr. Pittman clapped his hands, and Lauren spun around to face forward.

"Before the bell goes for recess," said Mr. Pittman, "I want to talk to you about a little competition." He paused to make sure he had everyone's attention. "As you know, every year the sixth- and seventh-grade classes have a special assembly in the last week of school."

A ripple of whispers ran through the class. Mr. Pittman waited until everyone was silent. "This year I would like to do something a little bit different." He looked around the room. "For this project, I want each of you to observe your family, your friends and maybe even your own heart, and then write about what you see and feel."

The class groaned. Mr. Pittman held up his hand for quiet. "It can be as long or as short as you wish. It can be in the form of a poem or a short story or even a play. And you can work alone or in pairs or groups. As long as you show me what is important to you."

He gazed around the class again, but this time there was no need to ask for quiet. "Mrs. Dupont and I will read them and choose the best one to present at the special assembly."

Lauren remembered that Mrs. Dupont was the librarian they'd met when they'd come for their tour.

"We can talk more about this later," Mr. Pittman finished.

The bell rang, and it was as if a spell had been broken. Suddenly the class was buzzing with noise. Alicia and Alex looked at each other, then rose together and made a dash for the door. Lauren put away her pencils and closed her notebook. She wondered if they were all dreading this assignment as much as she was. Writing was hard enough. Writing about personal stuff? Way too hard.

"Lauren!"

Lauren saw Callie waving to her from across the room. As she hurried over, she could feel Byron staring after her.

"Come hang out with us," said Callie, heading out the door. "Maddy! Treena! Wait up."

Lauren and Callie pushed their way through the crowd and caught up to the two other girls at the top of the stairs.

"Hey, guys," said Callie. "This is Lauren."

"We know." One of the girls, her lashes thick and heavy with mascara, looked Lauren up and down. "I'm Katreena Peterson," she finally said. "And this is Madeleine Chan."

"Maddy," said the other girl. "Madeleine sounds like something out of a soap opera." Her dark eyes crinkled when she smiled. "Where are you from?" she asked Lauren as they made their way down the stairs.

"I'm from Ash Creek," said Lauren. "In Saskatchewan."

"Never heard of it," said Maddy.

"It's pretty small. About two thousand people, I think."

Maddy made a noise, looking back at Lauren with a sneer. "Well, welcome to civilization," she said. "I'm sure you'll like living in the city."

Lauren smiled but wasn't really sure what Maddy meant by that. It sounded a bit mean.

"I went to the country once," said Treena. "To this tiny place in Ontario where my cousins live. I've never been so bored in my life. All they wanted to do was climb trees and swim in the lake and ride horses and stuff. And the hole they called a town..." She made a face. "It didn't even have a movie theater."

"It's different, that's for sure," said Lauren. She followed the girls out to the playground, a funny feeling settling in her stomach that had nothing to do with being hungry. She thought about her friends back home, Kat and Gemma and Isabel, and how nice they'd been to Lauren's cousin when she'd visited from Australia the previous year. They hadn't made her feel bad for where she came from.

They found a spot under a tree, and Lauren settled on the grass next to Callie. "I've got a chocolate bar, if anyone wants to share it with me," she said, pulling it out of her pocket.

Treena's nose wrinkled. "I don't eat that kind of stuff," she said. "Do you know how many calories are in that thing?"

"Well, I do," said Maddy, surprising Lauren by reaching over and taking it from her. "And this kind is my favorite." She ripped open the packaging and bit off almost a third of it, closing her eyes while she chewed. "I haven't had one of these in months." She passed the bar on to Callie.

"So what did you do out there in the wilderness?" asked Treena. "And please don't tell me you had horses or pet pigs or something."

Lauren bit her lip. "No. We didn't have any animals. We lived in town." She nervously picked at the grass. "I did dance and piano lessons and hung out with my friends. We'd go to movies and stuff."

"Beauty. You're semi-normal then," said Treena. She laughed, but it wasn't a happy sound.

"Alicia and Alex are from the country," said Callie through a mouthful of chocolate. "And are they ever screwed up."

Lauren squinted at her, surprised by the tone of her voice. "I mean, I know they're twins and all," Callie continued, "but they hardly even speak. It's like one of them thinks something and the other one does it. How weird is that? I have twin brothers, and they don't do that. I think it's got something to do with living on that ranch. They never had anyone to talk to but the cows."

"Callie, you're so full of it," said Maddy. She grabbed the chocolate bar back from Callie, took another bite and handed the remains to Lauren.

Lauren stared at the gooey blob of chocolate. She couldn't have swallowed it if she'd wanted to. Alicia and Alex had been really nice to her. She didn't

understand why Callie was being so
mean.

She looked up and saw a woman
wheeling Will toward the swings on
the other side of the playground. Will
spotted her and waved.

"Look at that kid," said Treena.
"What a spaz."

Lauren brought her hand down in
mid-wave and spun around to look at
Treena.

"I thought they weren't going to let
kids like that in anymore," said Maddy.

"Why? What do you mean, kids like
that?" Lauren asked.

Treena leaned in close to Lauren
and lowered her voice. "There used
to be this kid here that was kind of—
you know." She rolled her eyes and
gestured rudely with her hands. "No
one ever paid him much attention, but
one day he just went ape. Threw a total
fit, knocked over a bunch of chairs,

tried to bash the door down. Mr. Blight got punched in the face before they got him under control." She shuddered. "They tried to cover it up, said he'd missed his meds or something, but a bunch of parents complained and made sure they got rid of him."

"But that was just one incident," Lauren said, horrified. "Not all kids with disabilities are—"

"Are you saying they should have let him stay?" Treena glared at her. "Let him hang around until he started beating up on the kids in his class?"

"One outburst doesn't mean—"

"My brother was in that class, and it really freaked him out." Treena nodded over at Will. "I tell you, those kids are dangerous."

Lauren looked helplessly over at her brother, now being pushed on the swing by a couple of kids not much bigger than him.

"But he's only little," she said.

"He'll grow up."

Something in Treena's voice made Lauren look back at her. The fear and hatred Lauren saw in her face was frightening.

Chapter Five

Over the next couple of weeks Lauren fell into a routine. In some ways it felt as if she'd been at Birch Park Elementary for months.

Nothing was the same as it had been in Ash Creek though. She was no closer to having a friend than she had been on the first day. She hung out with Callie and Maddy and Treena sometimes, but she didn't really fit in. Their conversations were boring. All they ever talked about were clothes and makeup, boys and how many "likes" they got on social media. That boy Byron McAfee had still barely said a word to her and the twins…well, they were nice enough, but they really seemed to need only each other for company. Most days Lauren spent recess and lunch wandering the playground on her own, watching other kids and wishing the bell would ring.

On Saturday morning she lay in bed, fiddling with the locket that held the picture of her three friends. What had they been doing these last two weeks? Had they gone to the Busted Nugget for milkshakes on the last day of the holidays like they usually did? Had Isabel taken Lauren's place in the dance routine for the concert coming up? Were they planning a party for Valentine's Day? Did they miss her?

She sighed and threw the covers off, climbing out of bed.

Will was in the kitchen, his face smeared with porridge and jam. Her mom was washing up his bowl at the sink.

"Hey, Will," Lauren said, ruffling his hair as she passed on her way to the fridge.

He grinned at her and squeezed his fists tight.

She poured some orange juice into a glass. "Want to go to the park later?"

"Blake!" said Will.

It was a new word for him. Lauren frowned.

"Will has a play date today," explained her mom.

"A play date? With who?"

"A boy in his class. One of the first graders."

"Blake!" said Will again, squirming in excitement.

Lauren swallowed. So Will had made friends. Wow. She wished she could say the same. "That's great," she said, her voice a bit flat.

Her mom glanced at her. "Why don't you come along? I think Blake has a sister about your age."

Lauren groaned. "Mom, I'm not five anymore. You can't just dump me on some girl and expect us to be instant friends."

"And you can't expect to make friends if you don't make an effort." Her mom wiped Will's face with a cloth. "Think about it. You can come along and help me get Will's chair up the stairs. Then, if you don't want to stay, you can come home. They only live next door."

"Next door?" Lauren glanced out the kitchen window toward the neighbor's house. She'd heard what sounded like a whole army of kids playing in the backyard, but she hadn't seen any of them yet. No one seemed to be around now.

Lauren finished her juice and set the glass in the sink. "All right," she said. "I'll give you a hand with Will. But I'm coming home if it gets weird."

The neighbor's house was tall and rambling, larger than their own and in need of a coat of paint. A woman answered the door, her face breaking into a smile when she saw them. She introduced herself as Bernice.

"Gareth will be back with the other kids soon," she said as she led them down the hall to the kitchen. "The twins' soccer match wasn't quite finished so they stayed to cheer them on."

"Blake!" said Will as a small boy with blond hair leaped up and ran over to him. Lauren had seen the boy before, on the playground at school with Will.

Lauren picked at her nails as her mom transferred Will to the floor and Bernice bustled around getting cups from the cupboard.

"The others won't be long," Bernice said, peering out the kitchen window. "In fact, there they are now."

The front door squeaked open, and Lauren heard voices in the hallway. A small boy came running into the kitchen.

"They won, Mom, they won!" he shouted as three older boys followed him in. Two of them looked so much alike that Lauren couldn't help staring. Five boys! No wonder they sounded like an army from her house.

"Well done, you two," Bernice said, giving the twins a hug. "Everyone, this is Will and—"

"Lauren!"

Lauren turned to see two more people standing at the entrance to the kitchen. A tall, thin man and a girl with her ball cap on backward. It was Callie.

Chapter Six

Callie seemed genuinely pleased to see Lauren. Then she noticed Will on the floor with Blake. Her gaze went from Will to Lauren, and her smile faded. A small frown furrowed her brow.

"You two girls know each other?" asked Bernice.

"Lauren's the new girl in my class I was telling you about," said Callie.

"Of course, we should have realized," said Bernice. "Well, I'm sure you lot are starving. Jack, Andrew, get out of the pantry. I'll get some sandwiches going."

The boys slouched into the family room, the older three draping themselves on the couch, the small boy, Liam, on the floor with Blake and Will. Callie came and sat at the table with Lauren and her mother.

"I didn't know you had a brother," she said, watching Blake, Will and Liam setting up a board game.

Lauren shrugged. "I didn't know you had so many brothers."

Callie didn't reply. The two moms continued to chat while Bernice loaded the table with sandwich fixings: bread, cheese, ham, lettuce, tomatoes, peanut butter and jam. Lauren felt her face going hot as she thought about what Treena and Maddy had said about Will on that first day. And how Callie hadn't

42

said anything when Lauren tried to defend him.

"I should go," she said, pushing her chair back.

Callie looked up. "What? But you just got here."

Lauren shrugged.

"Don't go yet," said Callie. "Want to see my room? I just got some new Taylor Swift posters."

Taylor Swift wasn't really Lauren's kind of music, but Callie was being super friendly, like she had been that first time Lauren met her. She nodded.

"I can't believe you live next door," said Callie as they sat on her bed, flipping through magazines and eating sandwiches. "Mitchell used to live there. He moved to Ottawa last month. But I'd way rather have you next door. I've already got five brothers. I don't need another guy to hang out with."

"Five is a lot," said Lauren.

Callie nodded. "They are such a pain."

She scratched her fingernail on a perfume sampler in the magazine she was reading, brought it to her face and sniffed deeply. She made a face and set it down.

"So do you have any brothers or sisters? I mean, besides..." Callie gestured in the general direction of the kitchen, where they could hear the boys squealing and giggling.

"His name's Will," said Lauren. "And no, it's just the two of us." She stared at Callie, daring her to say something more.

Callie dropped her gaze and nodded, flipping pages. "Do you play soccer?" she asked after a minute.

Lauren let the tension ease out of her shoulders. She shook her head, glad Callie hadn't pushed, glad to be talking about something else. Now Callie knew that Will was her brother though. And there was no doubt she'd tell Maddy and Treena. It left a ball of anxiety in Lauren's gut.

"I've always done dance," she said. "I missed registration, though, so I won't be able to start at the new dance place until summer."

"I really wanted to play football," said Callie. "I played flag with Connor and the twins, but when they moved on to tackle, Mom and Dad said it was too rough and switched me over to soccer. I like it, but…it's not the same."

Lauren shrugged. "I've never really been into sports."

Callie laughed. "With five brothers I don't really have a choice. I've always been a bit of a tomboy. That's why it's so great to be hanging out with Maddy and Treena this year. Maddy plays soccer, but you'd never call her a tomboy. She even helped me redecorate my room over the holidays. Do you like it?"

Lauren gazed around at the pink walls, the soft white curtains, the fluffy cushions on the bed. It wasn't her style, but it looked really nice. "Yeah, it's great," she said.

"You hate it, don't you?" said Callie.

"No, I don't! It's great."

Callie leaned toward her. "To be honest, I'm still getting used to it. It's a bit too girly for me, but don't tell Maddy I said that." She laughed. "I used to have this whole collection of figurines on display. My shelves seem bare now."

Lauren looked over to where the magazines had been stacked next to a framed photo of Callie and Treena and Maddy. "There's plenty of room. You could still put some of them up there," she said.

"Nah. Maddy said they didn't go with the decor, and she's right. They would look out of place." She sighed wistfully. "I could show them to you, if you want."

"Yeah, let's see them," said Lauren.

Callie dragged a box out of the closet and started removing dozens of figurines. She had more than Lauren had ever seen outside a games store, including a couple that Lauren had on her own shelves at home.

"Do you like *Star Wars*?" Lauren asked, picking up a model of Chewbacca. It was one she was hoping to get for her birthday.

"Do I *like* it? It's only my favorite movie series of all time," said Callie. "I've got Yoda and Darth Vader too. They're in here somewhere." She dug around in the box until she found them.

"You should put them out if you love *Star Wars* so much," said Lauren.

"I've got Frodo and Pippin from *The Lord of the Rings* in my room."

"Do you?" Callie bit her lip and looked up at the shelf. "I guess one or two wouldn't hurt." She jumped up and placed the figures on the top shelf, then stood back to admire them. "Hey, that's not bad at all."

"I really like it," said Lauren.

Just then Will called out.

Callie looked at Lauren. "What does he want?"

"I don't know, but I'd better go see." Lauren got up and opened the bedroom door. Blake and Will were right outside. Will had a soccer ball on his lap.

"He wants to play kickball," said Lauren to Callie. "Maybe later," she said to Will.

His face fell, and a lump of guilt settled in Lauren's stomach.

"Ball!" demanded Will.

"We're busy," she said.

"How can he even play kickball?" whispered Callie, who had come up behind her. "I mean—"

Lauren shrugged. "He can kick. He just needs someone to drive his chair."

"Ball!" said Will again.

"Please?" said Blake. "Just for a bit."

Lauren looked at their eager faces, then back at Callie. "Want to?" she asked. "Just for a little while? I mean, it's not like we're doing much."

Callie bit her lip. "Okay, why not?" she said after a short pause. "I guess it's better than sitting around doing nothing."

Will threw up his hands in joy.

Outside, Callie marked the goals with some bricks they found under the porch. Blake kicked the ball toward Will, and Lauren steered his chair so he could catch it between his feet.

"Go for it," she whispered.

With a giggle, he let fly with his foot. Callie dodged for the ball, but it sped past her.

"Goal!" Blake shouted.

"A lucky shot," said Callie. "Okay, game on."

They kicked the ball back and forth for a while, laughing and stumbling about, until they started to get hungry again.

"You know, I've been thinking about that thing we have to write for Mr. Pittman," said Callie as they sipped lemonade at the kitchen table. "You know how I said I wanted to play football? Dad said there was no point when there really wasn't a future in it for girls. What about a story about a girl who *did* play football, and she wouldn't give it up? Maybe she pretended to be a boy or something, and then when she'd proved she was just as good as everyone else, they had to let her play."

"Hmm," said Lauren. "Not bad."

"I mean, it *is* an important thing in our family. Connor and the twins play football now, as well as soccer, and I think lots of girls would like to play. They just don't because girls aren't supposed to, you know? It's—like—trying to change people's attitudes, to accept things that aren't normal."

Lauren stared at her. Her gaze flicked back and forth, from Callie to Will. Changing people's attitudes. Hmm. Maybe Callie was onto something. "Sounds cool," she said.

"Do you want to work on it with me?" Callie asked.

"Yeah, maybe," said Lauren. "Hey, do you want to come to the pool with us tomorrow? I'm sure Mom wouldn't mind."

"Are you kidding?" said Callie. "Absolutely yes."

Lauren grinned, feeling lighter than she had for weeks.

Chapter Seven

"So I hear it's your birthday, Lauren," said Treena. She dropped onto a bench near the gym, and Maddy sat down next to her. Lauren and Callie were sprawled on the grass in front of them. The ground was wet from the rain, and Lauren could feel the damp seeping into her jeans.

"Yeah, how did you know?"

Treena smirked. "Word gets around. So you're thirteen?"

"Twelve."

Treena raised one perfectly shaped eyebrow. "Right. I forgot you're only in sixth grade."

Lauren shrugged. She stared off across the school playground. Will and Blake were near the monkey bars. Blake looked her way. Lauren shifted so her back was to them.

"Are you having a party?" said Maddy.

Lauren looked around. "No. I mean—not really."

Maddy tilted her head. "Callie said you were having a sleepover."

Lauren's gaze flew to Callie, who so far hadn't said a word. Callie looked away, her face flushed.

"Well, yeah," said Lauren. "Callie is going to sleep over. But it's not really a party. We're just going to watch all—"

Callie's gaze locked on hers, eyes wide.

"Watch what?"

"Movies," said Lauren quickly. "We're just going to watch movies." They'd both agreed a *Star Wars* marathon wouldn't be Maddy's and Treena's thing.

Maddy was staring intently at her. She nudged Treena with her elbow. "Sounds like fun, doesn't it, Treen?"

"Absolutely."

Lauren's stomach hurt. Her gaze moved from Maddy to Treena and then to Callie. She swallowed.

"I thought…I mean…"

Words tumbled around in her mind. She should invite them. Of course she should invite them. But she couldn't. The words formed in her head, but it was like there was a dam behind her throat. They wouldn't come out.

"My parents said I could only have one friend over," she blurted finally.

"I would have invited you. If they'd let me…" The lie trailed off unconvincingly.

Treena raised one eyebrow again. Maddy just stared.

Lauren shrugged. "You know how parents are."

Maddy's flat expression widened into a grin.

"Yeah, we know how parents are," she said. "Don't worry about it."

"Believe me, a twelve-year-old's birthday party wouldn't have been the highlight of my year," said Treena. She flicked her hair over her shoulder. "But we can't let your birthday go by without some sort of celebration, can we?" She looked around, then grinned at Maddy and Callie and stood up. "I know. Let's go to the 7-Eleven. I'll get you a Slurpee or a chocolate bar or something."

"Perfect," said Maddy, jumping up. "I'm starving."

"What?" said Lauren, clambering to her feet. "You mean now?"

"Sure, it's not far," said Treena.

Lauren looked over the fence toward the 7-Eleven on the other side of the park. Her heart started to thump.

"We're not supposed to leave the school grounds."

Treena rolled her eyes. "I knew she'd be too chicken to go for it."

"I'm not chicken," said Lauren.

"Then what's the problem?" Both of Treena's eyebrows were up this time, demanding an answer.

Lauren looked toward the playground. She thought she could hear Will laughing.

"Come on," said Callie. "It won't take long. We'll be back before anyone misses us."

"Unless we stand here talking about it for the next half hour," said Maddy, hands on her hips.

Lauren still hesitated, and Treena sighed dramatically. "Well, I'm going," she said, turning away. "Maddy? You coming?"

"You know it," said Maddy. They glanced around quickly and then ducked behind the gym.

"Come on, Lauren," said Callie. "We won't get in trouble. No one will know we've left." She took Lauren's hand and pulled her around the corner. "It's your birthday. They want to do something special for you."

Lauren let herself be dragged toward the edge of the school grounds. Her instinct was to go back, but Maddy and Treena had stopped at the gate. They were waiting for them.

"Are you coming or not?"

Lauren glanced over her shoulder. The sounds of the playground were dim. She couldn't hear any shouts or calls or voices yelling out for them.

Maybe no one would notice they were gone.

"All right," she said. "But we have to come straight back."

It wasn't far to the 7-Eleven, but Maddy and Treena seemed in no hurry. They slowed right down once they were out of sight of the school. Lauren trailed along behind them, listening to Callie's chatter, her palms sweaty and her heart racing.

The lady behind the counter didn't seem surprised to see them. In fact, she obviously knew Treena and asked how her brother was doing in high school. They chatted for a few minutes while Lauren stood shifting from foot to foot, biting the inside of her cheek.

"I haven't had one of these in ages," Maddy said once they were outside. She ripped off a chunk of the chocolate-covered donut she'd chosen and popped it into her mouth. Her eyes rolled back in appreciation.

"My dad makes amazing donuts," said Callie.

"Your dad's a pastry chef," said Maddy. "I've been to one of his Sunday brunches at The Grand. He makes great everything."

"That's true," said Callie, laughing.

Treena sipped her diet soda. "I don't know how you're not the size of a hippo, with a dad who's a pastry chef."

Callie shrugged. "It's not like he's making stuff at home all the time." She grinned. "We only get the rejects."

Lauren nibbled at the edge of her chocolate bar. Her throat felt tight, and it was hard to swallow. "Shouldn't we be getting back?" she said.

Treena pulled out her phone and checked the time. "I guess we should.

Don't want you to get detention on your birthday, do we?"

Maddy and Callie laughed, and Lauren smiled weakly. She was glad when they turned back up the hill toward the school.

The bell was ringing as they entered the gates, and they filed in with the rest of the kids, pushing their way through to make it up the stairs before Mr. Pittman. As she slipped into her seat, Byron McAfee gave her a long look. Then he lifted his hand and rubbed the corner of his lip slowly and deliberately.

Lauren touched her face. Her fingers came away covered in chocolate. She wiped the back of her hand across her lips, making sure all the evidence was gone. When she looked back, Byron had his head buried in a book. She took a deep breath and let it out slowly.

Chapter Eight

Lauren looked at the clock on the wall for the fifth time in as many minutes. One thirty. It was a dull, gray day, and Lauren felt about as dark as the sky she could see outside the classroom window. She'd been staring at the blank page in her notebook for the last twenty minutes. They were supposed to be working on their writing projects, but her brain was refusing to cooperate.

"Are you coming, Lauren?"

Lauren looked up to see Treena standing over her, Maddy and Callie on either side. She tried not to scowl. Ever since her birthday, seeing Treena reminded Lauren of the trip off the school grounds. And the lie she'd told her mom when she got home. It turned out Will had been looking for her during recess. He had wanted to sing "Happy Birthday" to her. He'd been practicing with Blake for days.

"Coming where?"

Treena rolled her eyes. "To the design presentation."

It was Career Day, and the school had organized several presentations and guest speakers. Maddy's mom was giving a speech about working at a law firm, and Callie's dad was doing a cooking demonstration. The fashion-design presentation was one of the most popular events. It was being organized by Treena's mom, who was a friend of the designer.

"Actually," said Lauren, "I thought I'd go to the library for the author talk." Callie was coming as well—at least, that's what they'd decided on the way to school that morning.

Treena raised her eyebrow. "The author talk? Are you a budding writer now too?" The way she said it did not sound like she was impressed.

Lauren flushed, her gaze flicking to Callie. "No. We—I mean, I just thought I might get some tips for our writing project."

"You're taking that thing way too seriously, Lauren," said Maddy. "Just scribble something down."

"It's not that easy."

"Come on, Lauren," said Callie. "They've set up a catwalk and everything. It'll be fun."

Lauren glared at her. They'd agreed to go to the author talk. Now Callie was backing out on her?

"Nah, I think I'll stick with the author thing," she said, looking down at her book. She was trying hard not to say something she would regret.

"She's a lost cause," said Maddy. "Let's go." She turned abruptly and walked away.

Callie hesitated for only a second, then followed Maddy and Treena out the door. Lauren stared after her.

What was going on? Callie and Lauren had agreed that the author talk would be a great way to get some ideas for their play. And they'd planned to work on it after school. Why was Callie going to listen to a fashion designer and watch girls strut around like Barbie dolls?

It wasn't like she had any interest in becoming a designer or a model or anything.

Lauren put away her pen and ruler and looked up to see Byron McAfee staring at her. She scowled at him. It was bad enough to be humiliated by her supposed best friend. She didn't need an audience as well. She slammed her notebook shut and packed up her stuff.

She didn't belong here. She'd known she wouldn't fit in even before they moved. She belonged at home in Ash Creek, with her friends. She should be going to Kat's after school, not to Callie's.

Lauren threw her backpack over her shoulder and stormed out of the classroom. She wanted to spin on the tire swing in Kat's front yard until she almost threw up. She wanted to have hot chocolate and cookies on Isabel's deck, and sleepovers at Gemma's. She wanted life to be normal again.

Lauren reached the bottom of the stairs and turned toward the library. At the end of the hallway, Will's class was filing outside, with Will at the head of the line, his chair being pushed by one of the other kids. Will's arms were flying about like a windmill gone haywire. At least someone's enjoying himself, she thought bitterly.

She sat through the author talk, trying to concentrate on what he was saying. He had some great stories about how he got his ideas. But her mind kept drifting. It was hard to put Callie out of her mind. She noticed that Byron was sitting on the other side of the library, taking notes. Great. She left as soon as the talk was over.

"Lauren!"

Lauren was tempted to keep going, but she stopped and waited for Callie to catch up.

"What do you want?" she asked, folding her arms across her chest.

"I thought we were going to work on the play," said Callie. "What's wrong?"

"What's wrong?" Lauren couldn't believe it. "How can you ask that?"

Callie frowned. "You're not mad about the author talk, are you?"

Lauren shook her head and marched down the hall.

"You are!" said Callie, trotting after her. "What's the big deal?"

Lauren kept walking. "We talked about it this morning," she said. "You promised you'd come to the author talk with me."

"Well, yeah...but Treena really wanted to go to the design presentation."

"So?" said Lauren. "No one was stopping her."

"I know, but..."

Lauren stopped and turned to face her. "But what?"

Callie bit her lip. "It was really important to her. Fashion is her thing, you know? Plus her mom organized it and everything. She wanted me to see it." She shrugged. "I thought you wouldn't mind, that you'd come too."

"To a *fashion* show? Really?"

"Sorry," said Callie. She actually looked sorry too.

Lauren sighed. "We really need to get going on that play. Do you still want me to come over?"

Callie's face brightened. "For sure."

"All right," said Lauren.

"Did you know that Treena was asked if she wanted to model for the presentation?" asked Callie, dodging as a kid ran past. "Only her mom wouldn't let her because she said Treena only takes jobs that pay, like the catalog shots she did last year."

It was as if Callie had completely forgotten everything that had happened. It wasn't quite as easy for Lauren. She couldn't help but think that Kat would never have let her down like that. Kat would have known she wouldn't be caught dead at a fashion parade. And she also would have known how important it was for her to do a good job on a school assignment.

They turned the corner, and Lauren saw Blake wheeling Will out of his classroom. He waved at them and headed in their direction.

"Come on," said Callie. "Let's go." She pulled her toward the exit.

Lauren opened her mouth to protest and then closed it again. Treena and Maddy were standing near the door. Maddy was talking to someone on her cell phone. She didn't look happy and turned her back when she saw them. Lauren hesitated, glancing back at Blake and Will. Her stomach clenched as she saw Blake speed up to catch them. She quickly turned and followed Callie out the door.

"See you tomorrow," Treena said as they walked by.

"Yeah, see ya," said Lauren. She'd never felt worse in her life.

Chapter Nine

Callie leaped down her front steps and ran over to Lauren, who had told her mom and Will to keep going up the hill to school. "Fifty dollars! Can you believe it?"

Lauren laughed. Callie was so excited. "What are you talking about?"

"I got fifty dollars for my birthday, from my nan," said Callie. "She always sends us money for our birthdays. Usually it's twenty dollars, and last year I bought that Chewbacca figure I have in my collection. But fifty!" She spun around and did a little dance. "I'm going to get some new jeans. I begged Mom to get me a cool pair I saw, but she bought me some cheap no-name ones instead. Said she wasn't going to spend all that money just for a label. Can you believe it?"

Lauren shook her head. "If I had fifty dollars, I wouldn't be spending it on a pair of jeans."

"But these ones are so in," said Callie. "Maddy wears them all the time. They look awesome."

"Yeah, but Maddy's stepdad is super rich. You can bet she didn't spend her own money on them," said Lauren.

Callie shrugged. "Probably not. But still, she always looks amazing. I have to have them. Want to come to the mall with me on Saturday? I want to get them before my party. And we could go to that comic shop afterward."

"That sounds like fun," said Lauren.

A door slammed behind them, and Lauren turned to see some of Callie's brothers racing down the stairs. Blake was at the back of the pack, but he pushed past the twins and ran ahead. Lauren watched him race up the hill, his backpack bouncing wildly, only stopping when he'd caught up to Will.

Seeing them, the lump in Lauren's stomach grew just a little bit, as it did each time she saw them at school and chose to ignore them. She turned away and tried to concentrate on what Callie was saying.

Saturday afternoon, Lauren was back in front of Callie's house. She knocked on the door.

"Bad news," Callie said when she answered. "Mom says we have to take Blake to the mall with us. The boys have gone to a football game with Dad, but Blake hates football. And now Mom's sick and she's going to the doctor, but Blake can't stay here by himself." She sighed.

Lauren shrugged. "That's okay. Mom said I have to take Will too." She gestured to where she'd left Will in his chair at the bottom of the steps.

Will grinned up at Callie and waved.

Callie waved at him. "Maybe this isn't such a good idea," she said.

Just then Blake came to the door. "Yes! Will's coming too?"

Lauren nodded, and Blake bounded down the steps.

Callie shook her head. "Brothers," she said. "Come on. Let's go."

Lauren let Blake push Will's chair and followed behind with Callie.

Callie was unusually quiet, and for once Lauren found herself searching for something to talk about.

Blake and Will stopped at the entrance to the school.

"Will wants to play on the playground," Blake said.

Callie rolled her eyes. "You mean *you* do."

"No, Will does," insisted Blake.

Will pointed toward the school and said, "Play!"

"We can't stop at the playground, Will," said Lauren. "We're going to the mall, remember?"

"Swing!" said Will.

"Just for a minute?" asked Blake. "The tire swing is awesome."

"The tire swing?" said Lauren. "I thought he was only allowed on the one they adapted for him. Is it safe? He can't hold on very well, you know."

"We go on it all the time, don't we, Will?" said Blake. "Come on. I'll show you." He pushed Will onto the school grounds, and Lauren and Callie followed. "Ms. Westhaven or Miss Chatwal usually lifts him on. Can you do it?" Blake asked.

Lauren unstrapped Will and transferred him onto the swing so his legs hung over the edge and his bum sagged into the hole. Will wiggled in excitement, and she held on tight.

"See, I told you he can't hold on," she said.

"He doesn't need to," said Blake. "I hold on to him."

He grabbed the chains of the swing and hoisted himself on, sitting on the edge of the tire and wrapping his legs around Will's body. Then he started pumping.

Lauren watched as they swung back and forth.

"Not too high," she said, immediately regretting the words. She sounded like Mr. Burman.

Will laughed out loud, and Lauren felt a pang of jealousy. She'd always been the one to make Will laugh, the one to play games with him, make him squeal in delight. Now here she stood on the sideline, telling Blake to be careful.

She looked over at Callie, who was swinging alongside them, giggling almost as much as Will.

"Come on, Lauren," she called. "Bet you can't jump from this high." She gave an extra-hard push and then leaped from the swing, landing gracefully on her feet.

Lauren turned away. "Nah. Let's get to the mall."

She dragged Will off the tire swing, and they headed out the gate. Callie seemed to have shaken off her glum mood and chatted away about her birthday party.

"It's a sleepover," she said, "and Mom's going to help me make these cool invitations that look like sleeping bags. I was going to get the *Harry Potter* movies, but I'm not sure Maddy and Treena would be into that. What kind of movies do you think they would like?"

Lauren shrugged.

"And Dad's going to make us a Sunday brunch because it's his day off. Treena's never tasted Dad's cooking. She's going to flip."

They arrived at the mall and went straight to the jeans shop.

"Aren't they gorgeous?" Callie said, holding up a pair of black skinny-leg jeans.

"How much are they?" said Lauren.

Callie looked at the tag, and her face fell. "Eighty-five. On sale. I only have fifty."

As if by magic, a salesclerk appeared beside them.

"They're beautiful, aren't they?" she said. "We've hardly been able to keep them stocked. All the girls are wearing them." She looked Callie up and down. "Would you like to try them on? I think we have your size."

Callie shook her head. "No, I haven't got enough money," she said.

"I can put them on hold for you, if you don't have the money with you today," said the girl. "Why don't you try them on?"

Lauren followed Callie to the changerooms, leaving Will and Blake just outside, where she could see them from the door.

"Are you sure about this?" she asked as Callie slipped the jeans on and admired herself in the mirror. "Where are you going to get the rest of the money?"

"It's only thirty-five more. I could do some weeding or something to make it up," she said.

"But—*eighty-five* dollars for a pair of jeans? You could get a new Xbox game or buy a speaker for your room."

"I don't need a speaker. I've got headphones." Callie took the jeans off and folded them carefully. "You don't understand. *I have* to have these jeans."

"Okay," said Lauren. "It's your money."

Callie asked the salesclerk to put the jeans on hold, and they left the shop.

"We may as well go home," she said. "I can't afford to spend any money on comics."

"That's all right," said Lauren, reaching into her purse. "Here. Mom gave me ten dollars for each of us."

"Wow, that's cool," said Callie, pocketing the bill. "Your mom's really nice."

"She was just feeling guilty about making me bring Will along. I won't complain though."

They took the elevator to the second floor, where the comic shop was located. As they made their way toward the entrance, Callie's chatter suddenly stopped mid-sentence. She grabbed Lauren's arm and spun her around, steering her toward a coffee shop on the other side of the mall.

"What's wrong?" said Lauren, looking back toward the shop.

Callie's face was flushed. She looked at Lauren and then away. "Maddy and Treena are in there."

Chapter Ten

The words hit Lauren like a bowling ball to the stomach.

"I forgot," Callie said, turning brighter and brighter shades of red. "I told them we'd meet them here after I got my jeans." She glanced at Will. "You know how Treena is, Lauren." Her eyes were pleading with Lauren to understand. "We can't go in there."

The bowling ball rolled around in Lauren's stomach. She glanced at Will, squirming with anticipation, pointing in the direction of the comic shop. "Why don't we go and get an ice cream, Will?" she said.

Will shook his head firmly. "Comic!" he said.

"You can have mint chip. It's your favorite."

Will frowned. "Comic."

"I think he wants to go to the comic shop," said Blake.

"I know what he wants," Lauren snapped. She could see Treena through the window of the comic shop.

"No," she said. "No comics. Let's go."

She took the handles of Will's chair and headed back toward the elevator. She looked back and realized Callie wasn't following her.

"So…I'll see you on Monday?" said Callie.

Lauren's eyes widened. "You're not coming with us?"

Callie's face flamed bright red again. She looked at the floor somewhere near Lauren's feet. "Well, I promised I'd meet them…you know, and…I can't just not show up."

"So you're *ditching* us?"

Callie lifted her gaze. "No, I mean—" She bit her lip and shot a look back over her shoulder. "I'm sorry, Lauren. I've got to go."

Grabbing Blake's sleeve, she dragged him over to the other side of the mall, disappearing into the comic shop.

Lauren stood there, her hands clenched tightly on the handles of Will's chair. She felt like the floor had dropped out from under her. The world was spinning, and she didn't know if she was going to come out on top or not. Then everything seemed to grind to a halt, and she glared at the spot where Callie had disappeared. Fine. If Callie would rather be with Maddy and Treena, she could have them.

Lauren spun Will's chair around so hard that it tipped up on two wheels. Inside the elevator she stabbed the button for the ground floor, tapping her foot impatiently. How could she have been so stupid? She'd thought Callie was her friend. She'd thought she could count on her when she needed her, but all Callie wanted was to hang out with her *cool* friends. The doors opened and she stormed out. She didn't need friends like that. Friends like that weren't friends at all.

Will called out, and she realized she'd almost passed the ice-cream shop.

"Ice cream!" said Will.

She paid for the ice cream. That's when she realized that Callie still had the money she'd given her, and it made her even angrier.

"Is that mint-chip?" she heard a voice ask behind her. The voice sounded familiar. Lauren turned to find Byron leaning close to Will, comparing cones.

"Byron?"

He straightened up and stared at her. "Lauren. Hi." His brows came down in a puzzled frown, and he looked from her to Will and back again. "Are you with Will?"

"Yeah. He's—he's my brother," she said. It felt strange to say it. She hadn't told anyone at school that they were related. "You know Will?"

"I help out in the library. Will comes in with his friends to use the computer."

Another thing Lauren didn't know about Will.

"He's your brother, eh?" Byron continued. "Funny, I've never seen you guys together at school."

Lauren's cheeks burned. "Well, I'm usually pretty busy, you know, with… things."

There was an awkward pause, and then Byron shrugged. "Well, I have to go," he said. He bent down and saluted Will with his cone. "See you at school, Will. Enjoy your ice cream."

Lauren watched him walk off until he was lost in the crowd. He had never said more than a couple of words to her before.

"Oh!" said Will from behind her.

Lauren turned to find an empty cone in his hand and the ball of chocolate-flecked green ice cream lying on the floor next to his chair.

"Oh, Will," she said. She bought him another ice cream, pushed the scoop deep into the cone with a plastic spoon and handed it to him. "Time to go home, buddy."

Chapter Eleven

Monday morning came around, and Lauren was still furious. For the first time in weeks, she left the house early and walked to school with her mother and Will. Since she had fifteen minutes to spare, she decided to go to the library. It didn't take her long to choose a fantasy novel. She made her way to the checkout desk, where she saw a familiar face. Byron.

"Hi, Lauren," he said.

"Hey," she said, searching for her name on the computer and scanning her book. When she turned around, Byron was still standing there. She couldn't read his face. Was he thinking about her and Will?

"Is that *The Knights of Gandor*?" he asked, turning his head sideways to read the title.

Quickly she hid the book behind her back. "What do you care?"

He shrugged. "It's a good book."

"You've read it?" said Lauren.

"About fifty times." He laughed. "I think I've got it memorized."

Lauren laughed too. "I've only read it three times, but it is great, isn't it?"

The bell rang, and Byron looked up. The smile left his face.

"We'd better get to class," said Lauren.

Byron didn't say a word as they climbed the stairs to the second floor and walked down the hallway to room 215. Lauren began to think she'd imagined the smile on his face. Callie was already in her seat next to Treena. Her eyes widened when she saw Lauren and Byron together.

Lauren flushed and turned away. Callie wasn't her friend anymore, so what did she care who Lauren hung out with?

When Lauren went downstairs for breakfast the next morning, there was an envelope waiting for her on the table.

"It was in the mailbox," said her mom.

Lauren peeled the flap open carefully and pulled out the card inside.

It was an invitation to Callie's birthday party. It was shaped like a sleeping bag. *It's party time!* Lauren could hear Callie's voice shouting those words in her head as she read it. She pressed her lips together and scowled.

"Who is it from?" said her mom.

Lauren stuffed the invitation back into the envelope. "No one. It's nothing."

She watched her mom feeding Will his oatmeal with applesauce. He grinned up at her.

"Play Will," he said.

"Sure," she said after a slight hesitation. Her fingers tightened on the envelope. "Want me to push you on the swing at recess?"

Will shook his head.

"Blake!" he said. He pointed to a picture on his communication board that showed *afternoon* and said, "Laurie."

Now Will didn't want to hang out with her at school.

"Okay, after school," she said. She went back upstairs to finish getting ready.

There was the usual lineup of cars in the drop-off zone in front of the school when they arrived. Lauren had the door half-open when she saw Maddy getting out of a BMW. Maddy slammed the car door hard and flung her bag over her shoulder, stalking away without a backward glance. She headed straight for Lauren.

Lauren froze, one hand on the door, watching her approach. Her heart started to thud. At the last minute she wrenched the door open just as Maddy reached her.

Maddy paused, staring her down. Her eyes were red, her face crumpled by a frown. "What are you gawking at?" she said.

"I wasn't—I was just—"

Maddy shook her head and continued through the door without another word. Lauren let it fall closed behind her.

Then she spotted Callie and Treena walking toward her from the other direction. She ducked inside quickly and darted up the stairs.

Still unwilling to face Callie, Lauren wandered over to the back field at lunchtime to watch a group of younger kids playing soccer. They were fun to watch, running after the ball in a pack and kicking it back and forth with no real strategy. After a few minutes she saw Will heading out onto the field. Blake was pushing his wheelchair. Lauren's chest squeezed tight as the game started up again. She watched the two of them chase after the ball, Will's chair bumping along the grass like a monster truck. Blake caught the ball between Will's feet, and Will gave it a kick. It sailed over the heads of his opponents, just missing the goal.

"Nice try, Will!" Ms. Westhaven called from the sidelines.

Lauren glanced over at her, then back at Will and Blake. They were moving back into position while the goalkeeper retrieved the ball. She bit her lip as the ball was kicked in Will's direction and Blake took off after it again, then closed her eyes and turned away. The lump had settled in her stomach again and sat there like a stone.

She trudged aimlessly around the playground, watching other kids running and screaming and laughing, until she realized she was holding *The Knights of Gandor*. She'd finished it the night before and planned on returning it to the library. As she crossed the field and headed toward the building, she saw Callie, Treena and Maddy sitting under a tree. She put her head down and went the long way around to the back entrance.

A burst of laughter followed her as she rounded the corner. Trying to block the sound from her ears, she yanked the door to the library open with such force that she almost knocked over a little girl coming out carrying several picture books.

Lauren murmured an apology and dropped her book into the return slot. This was getting way out of hand. She couldn't avoid Callie and the others forever. She would have to face them sooner or later.

She couldn't force herself to do it right then though. Wandering over to find a new book, she noticed Byron standing in the fantasy section, a stack of books at his feet.

"Finished *The Knights of Gandor*?" he said when she approached.

"Yeah." She plucked a book off the shelf and started reading the back cover.

"Have you read *Angels at Dusk*?"

Lauren looked at the book he was holding out to her.

"No, is it any good?"

"If you liked *The Knights*, you'll love this one," said Byron. "It's Marg Tessler's new one."

The bell rang. They'd just turned to go back to class when Lauren heard a commotion at the front of the library. It was Blake. He was trying to talk to Mrs. Dupont but was breathing so hard he could barely get the words out.

"Lauren!" he called as he spotted her. "I've been looking all over for you. Will's had an accident."

Lauren stared at Blake, her mouth open. There was blood on his shirt. Will's blood? Panic surged through her like electricity.

"What happened? Where's Will?"

"He's in the medical room. He got hit with the ball and his chair tipped over. There was blood everywhere.

He was crying and I couldn't find you and…" Blake hiccuped, and tears started running down his face.

Byron patted him on the back. "It's all right, Blake. You've found her now."

Byron's calm words seemed to set Lauren's brain into action. She was suddenly able to feel her limbs again. She pushed past him and raced for the medical room.

Chapter Twelve

Lauren ran down the hallway, ignoring the stares of kids starting to move back to their classrooms. When she neared the medical room, she could hear Will crying.

"It's all right, Will. It's all right, I'm here," she said when she got there, cuddling him and stroking his hair. "You're going to be all right." But she wasn't sure he was going to be all right. There was blood everywhere. Down his shirt, on the bed, on the floor. Mrs. Wallace, the first-aid attendant, was holding a cloth to Will's face with gloved hands, but there was blood on her dress. Lauren's insides turned to ice.

She heard the sound of a siren, and then the paramedics were there, gently prying her away from him. They quickly transferred him to a stretcher.

She heard Mrs. Wallace speaking quietly to them. "Yes, his mother has been contacted."

Lauren followed them out to the parking lot. Their murmuring voices seemed to be coming from a long way off. She was dimly aware that Byron and Blake were still there, following along on either side of her.

The paramedics put Will into the ambulance just as Lauren's mother drove up.

"Mom!" Lauren ran to her, and suddenly tears were running down her cheeks.

Lauren's mom spoke to the paramedics for a moment, then took Lauren by the shoulders and leaned down so they were face to face.

"Lauren," she said firmly. "Will's had an accident, but he's going to be fine."

"But—but the blood—there's so much—"

"Lauren. I need you to do something for me. It's very important."

Lauren stopped crying and sniffed loudly.

"I need to go to the hospital with Will, and I need you to stay here. I need to know that you're okay. Do you understand?"

Lauren nodded and wiped her nose on her sleeve.

"Go home with Callie after school.

Your dad or I will pick you up there later. Bernice will look after you. Can you do that?"

Lauren sniffed and nodded again.

"Good girl." Her mom gave her a quick hug, and then she was gone.

Lauren watched her mom drive out of the parking lot, following the ambulance. She felt like she'd never see them again. Then an arm came around her shoulders and pulled her away.

"Come on, dear," said Mrs. Wallace. "Don't worry about your brother. He's in good hands. Now let's get you cleaned up."

Half an hour later Lauren eased the door to her classroom open and tried to slip in unnoticed. But the latch closed with a resounding *CLICK*. Mr. Pittman looked up.

"Lauren Scanlon, you're late," he said. Twenty-six pairs of eyes swiveled in her direction.

"I'm sorry, Mr. Pittman," said Lauren, feeling raw and exposed in the faded shirt she'd borrowed from the lost-and-found box. She handed him the note Mrs. Wallace had given her and waited while he read it.

"Oh, so that's what that was all about," said Mr. Pittman. "I'm sorry, Lauren. Please take your seat."

"Are you okay?" whispered Byron as she took the seat next to him. Alicia and Alex were watching her with matching looks of concern on their faces.

"Yeah, sure," said Lauren. But she was cold all over, and every time she thought about the blood pouring from Will's face, she started shivering.

She sat through her science and art classes as if she were lost in a fog. What was happening at the hospital?

Was Will all right? When would he be coming home? She kept her eyes on the clock, watching the hands drag slowly forward.

Finally the bell rang, and she shoved her books into her desk. She looked over at Callie. She hadn't spoken to her for three days. How was she going to ask if she could go home with her? Callie had put her things into her backpack and was following Treena and Maddy to the door.

Lauren hurried to catch up.

"Callie." Her voice came out in a hoarse croak, and she cleared her throat. "Callie!"

Callie stopped and turned toward her. Maddy and Treena did as well.

"What do *you* want?" asked Treena, looking down her nose at Lauren.

Lauren's throat dried up. She thought she might be sick. "Nothing. I just need to talk to Callie."

"We know all about your little secret," said Maddy.

"My—my secret?"

"Yeah. We saw you at the mall with that kid. Callie filled us in. He's your brother?" Maddy's eyebrows were raised, her look a cross between scorn and amusement.

"Yeah, he's my brother." Lauren's eyes darted over to Callie. "That's what I wanted to talk—"

"So what's wrong with him?" asked Treena. "Did the doctor drop him on his head or something, or do gimps just run in the family?" She sniggered. "Now I know why you sit at that table with the other freaks. You all have gimps in your families."

Lauren stared, mouth open, unable to believe her ears.

"Look at her," said Treena. "It must be catching—she's starting to look like him."

Something exploded inside Lauren's head. She snapped her jaw closed and glared at Treena.

"I'd rather be like him than you any day," she said. "He's got more caring and spirit and joy and fun in him than you'll ever have. And he's got friends, real friends, who care about him and look out for him and don't abandon him because other people are too narrow-minded and bigoted to give him a chance." She looked at Callie when she said this. "He's my brother, and I love him, and no one's ever going to take that away from me."

She turned and stumbled through the door, dashing angry tears away with the back of her hand. She heard Callie calling her name, but she didn't care. She flew down the stairs and out the door at the bottom and ran.

Chapter Thirteen

Lauren didn't know where she was going. She just knew she had to get away. Get away from Treena and Maddy and Callie. Get away from the visions of blood that refused to leave her head. Get away from her thoughts about Will and the way she'd been treating him the last couple of months. Especially that.

She let her feet take her where they would, leaping over curbs, racing through the grass, pounding on pavement until finally her lungs couldn't keep up with them anymore. She fell back to a walk and then stopped altogether as her legs started to quiver.

Exhausted, she hunched down on the sidewalk to catch her breath. She had no idea where she was. The buildings around her were unfamiliar. She knew this should worry her, but she didn't feel anything. She was numb.

She wandered aimlessly, not caring which way she turned, passing parks and gas stations, half-empty parking lots and even a school. A dog ran out from behind a fence, barking furiously. She dodged out of the way, narrowly missing being hit by a car. The driver blasted his horn at her, and she jumped back onto the sidewalk. Still she kept walking.

She thought about the day they'd spent at the pool. They'd had so much fun. She and Will and Callie and Blake. She had thought she'd found a friend. Someone who could accept her for who she was and accept Will as her brother. But she'd been wrong. Now Will was hurt, and she might never be able to tell him she was sorry.

She rested her forehead on the cold metal of a signpost. Of course you'll be able to tell him, she told herself. He'll be fine. He's probably on his way home now. But another voice in the back of her head whispered that maybe he wasn't. Maybe his injury was worse than her mom had let on. Maybe she'd never get a chance to talk to him again.

She stood there for a long time. She'd forgotten her jacket at school, and she shivered in the cold wind. The dried sweat on her back was like a layer of frost covering her body.

She had to admit that she was lost.

She turned a corner, and then another, looking for something familiar now, something that would point the way home. At last she spotted the lights of a 7-Eleven up ahead and darted inside.

"You all right, love?" asked the cashier.

Lauren shook her head, taking deep, gulping breaths.

"All right, just take it easy." The woman came around from behind the cash register. Lauren noticed a rose tattoo on her forearm. She sounded Scottish. For some reason Lauren found that comforting. "Are you hurt? Do you need an ambulance?"

"No—no," said Lauren, still short of breath. "I'm just—I'm lost."

"You poor dear," the woman said, patting Lauren's shoulder awkwardly. "Don't worry—we'll get you home."

Lauren's breathing slowed, and she wiped the tears from her cheeks.

"Where do you live?" said the woman.

Lauren told her the street name. "Is it far from here?"

"Not too far. Just go left at the light and all the way down Broadway. You'll see Birch Park Elementary on the right-hand side and—"

"That's my school."

"Then you know your way from there." The woman smiled, dimples appearing in her cheeks. "Hurry up now, lass," she said as Lauren turned to leave. "It'll be dark soon."

"Thank you."

The house was in shadows when Lauren finally arrived home. She found the spare key under the potted plant, let herself in and flicked the light on in the hallway.

"Mom? Dad?" she called out, but she already knew that no one was home.

The house had an eerie, empty feel to it. She checked the answering machine, but there were no messages. They weren't home. They hadn't tried to contact her. She was on her own.

She wandered around the house, through the living room with Will's empty standing frame in the corner, the kitchen with its three chairs and the empty spot where Will's wheelchair fit, into the dining room where the baby grand stood silent. Suddenly Lauren couldn't stand the stillness anymore. She ran up the stairs to her room and flung herself onto her bed, dragging the comforter over her head.

She didn't think she would sleep, but she must have, because she woke sometime later feeling stiff and cramped. She wasn't sure where she was at first. The room was dark and felt small and close around her. Then it all came flooding back. Will. Her parents must still be at the hospital.

The house was so quiet. Lauren focused on the soft ticking of the cuckoo clock on her wall. *Tick. Tick. Tick.* The seconds stretched longer and longer.

Just when Lauren thought she'd go crazy listening to the silence, she heard a car pull into the driveway. She threw the comforter off and peered out the window. Her dad's car. He was alone.

Don't panic, Lauren told herself. Everything's all right. But her heart was racing a mile a minute, and her hands and feet had suddenly turned to ice.

She jumped off the bed and tore down the stairs as the key grated in the lock.

"What's happening? Is Will all right? Tell me he's all right."

"He's fine, honey, he's fine."

Her dad hugged her and stroked her hair. Lauren found herself laughing and crying at the same time. She wiped her nose with her sleeve.

"He's really all right?"

"He will be," said her dad. "He broke his nose and lost a tooth. The doctor wanted to keep him in for observation."

Lauren sniffed loudly. "He looked so horrible. There was so much blood."

"Yes, I know," said her dad. "And he doesn't look much better now. He's going to have a couple of black eyes, but he's proud as punch he's finally lost his first tooth."

Lauren giggled, a wet, gurgling sound.

"But what are you doing here?" asked her dad. "Bernice said you didn't come home with Callie. We didn't know what to think. Then we rang here and you didn't answer—we were frantic."

"I'm sorry, Dad. But they were so horrible, saying mean things about Will. I just couldn't stand it."

"Who? Callie?" said her dad. "That doesn't sound like her."

"No, it wasn't Callie, it was Treena, but Dad, when Callie's around Treena and Maddy, she's different. She does whatever they want and goes along with whatever they say. I couldn't just stand there and take it."

"No, of course not." Her dad patted her on the shoulder. "It's all right. I'm just glad you're safe." He stood up. "Now we'd better call your mom. She'll be worrying."

Chapter Fourteen

The next morning Lauren went with her dad to the hospital to see Will. The familiar smell of disinfectant greeted her at the door. Memories flooded her of all the times she'd waited while Will underwent various tests and therapy sessions. But it had never been in an emergency. She had never experienced this nervous flutter of dread.

Peering through the doorway, she saw him lying in the bed nearest the door. He looked so small and fragile, his pale arms standing out against the bright-colored blanket. Huge bluish-black circles surrounded both eyes. His nose was taped, and his lips were red and swollen. Her heart squeezed tight.

Will spotted Lauren in the doorway and raised an arm to wave at her. "Lo!"

The tightness in Lauren's chest eased, and she smiled.

"Hey, Will," she said, moving to the bed. "How are you?"

He gave her a huge grin in answer and pointed to the gap in his teeth.

"Gone!" he said.

Lauren pretended to be surprised. "Wow! Did the tooth fairy come?"

Will nodded eagerly and held up his fist to show her the shiny coin he had clenched inside.

"*Two* dollars?" said Lauren. "Wow, she must really like you. I only ever got one."

Will grinned even harder, if that was possible.

The day passed slowly. Lauren's dad had to go to work, but Lauren and her mom didn't leave Will's side. Nurses came in once in a while to check Will's blood pressure and look into his eyes. Finally the doctor came in, gave him another look and said he was well enough to go home.

"Thank goodness for that," said Lauren's mom. She dressed Will and transferred him to his wheelchair.

As she followed her mom and Will down the hallway, Lauren noticed there was dried mud on the tires of his wheelchair from the soccer game.

"I guess you won't be playing soccer anymore," she said.

Will squirmed and nodded his head.

"Well, not for a while anyway," said their mom.

Lauren's mouth dropped open. "You're still going to let him play soccer? After all this?"

Her mom stopped to press the button for the elevator.

"It could have happened to anyone, Lauren. Risk of injury is part of the game."

"But it didn't happen to just anybody," said Lauren. "It happened to Will."

"And he will heal like anyone else." Her mom looked at Lauren long and hard. "We've never babied him, Lauren. You of all people should know that, and we're not going to start now."

"But—"

"Remember when you broke your toe at the dance recital a couple of years ago? We didn't make you stop dancing just because you hurt yourself." She sighed.

"Will loves soccer, Lauren, and if he wants to play, I'm not going to say no."

Will nodded his head and waved his arms enthusiastically.

"Play ball!" he cried.

Lauren looked at his battered face. No bruise could hide the eagerness shining out of his eyes.

"I guess you're right," she said.

They'd only just arrived home when the doorbell rang. Callie and Blake were standing on the front porch.

"Is Will okay?" asked Blake. "Is he home? Can I see him?"

"Yeah, he's in the kitchen. Go on in." Lauren moved aside, and Blake flew past.

There was an awkward silence. Lauren watched Callie as she stood staring at her feet, nervously scraping a bit of dirt off the doormat with the toe of her sneaker.

"Blake told me what happened," Callie finally said. "Is he okay?"

"No, he's got a broken nose, two black eyes and a missing tooth," said Lauren.

Callie raised her head, and Lauren saw that there were tears in her eyes.

"I'm so sorry, Lauren," she said. "I've been so awful. All I wanted was to be friends with Treena and Maddy. I thought if I was friends with the cool girls, it wouldn't be so bad going to high school and all. But I didn't mean to hurt your feelings. I don't think Will's a spaz like Treena said. I really like him. He's the best friend Blake's ever had, and you're the best friend I've ever had, and now I've gone and wrecked it and…"

She stopped. The silence stretched longer, but Lauren just waited, her heart beating fast. There was a lump in her throat.

"…and I'm just sorry. That's all,"

Callie finished. She looked at Lauren helplessly for a couple of seconds and then turned to go.

Lauren finally found her voice. "Callie." She swallowed, but the lump didn't move. "I'm sorry too."

"For what?"

"For not being honest about Will in the first place," she said. "He's my brother. I shouldn't have tried to hide that. And I'm not going to anymore."

Callie looked at her. "So can we start over?"

"What about Treena and Maddy?" Lauren asked.

Callie shrugged. "I don't think they'll want to hang out with me anymore."

"Why not?"

"Well…" A funny look came over Callie's face, like she didn't know whether to laugh or cry. "They were saying all these mean things about you after you left yesterday. So I told them where to go."

"You did?"

"Yeah." A huge grin split her face. "You should have seen Treena. She looked like she was going to explode." She giggled and shrugged again. "But I couldn't let them insult my best friend, could I?"

Lauren stood there, grinning at Callie, feeling happy and giddy and relieved and grateful all at the same time. The weight in her chest had lifted, and she felt so light she thought she might float away.

"Still friends?" asked Callie.

Lauren laughed. "Of course, silly." She grabbed Callie's arm and dragged her inside. "Come on. You should see Will. He looks like he did ten rounds with Muhammad Ali, but all he cares about is the money he got from the tooth fairy."

As soon as they entered the kitchen, Will pointed to the gap in his teeth. "No tooth!" he cried.

"Wow," said Callie. "Congratulations, Will." She turned to look at Lauren, her eyes like saucers.

Lauren did her best not to giggle.

The doorbell rang. Lauren heard the murmur of voices in the hallway. A moment later Dad came into the kitchen.

"Will, you've got another visitor," he said.

It was Byron. He kneeled beside Will's chair and placed a plastic shopping bag on Will's lap.

Will squirmed and giggled. "Cold," he said.

"It's just a little get-well present," said Byron, lifting the bag off Will's lap again. "Mint-chip. Your favorite, right?"

Will nodded. "Ice cream!"

"Here, I'll take that," said Mom. "I think there's enough for all of you. Will, you okay to share?"

Will nodded again. "Ice cream!"

Byron looked over at Lauren. "I was worried when you didn't come to school today. I wanted to make sure Will was all right."

"Thanks," said Lauren.

He glanced at Callie. "It reminded me a bit of last year when—you know—when that thing happened with my brother. It was so awful." He let his gaze fall to the table and then glanced at Will. "I just had to make sure he was okay."

Callie flushed pink, but she nodded.

"What thing? What happened to your brother?" asked Lauren.

"You know. That episode he had," said Byron. His gaze moved from Lauren to Callie and back again. "You mean you really don't know about it? I thought for sure Treena would have filled you in."

"She did tell you, remember?" said Callie. "On your first day. About that boy in Mr. Blight's class last year. The boy who…you know…"

Suddenly it all made sense to Lauren. Byron's silence in class, how he kept to himself. And his friendship with Will. He knew what it was like to be different. Lauren remembered Treena's comment about all the freaks at Lauren's table, and now, at last, she understood what she'd meant.

"That was your brother?" she said. "The one who had a meltdown and hit Mr. Blight?"

Byron nodded.

Lauren looked over at Will, wriggling in his seat, waiting for his ice cream. He was pretty easy-going, but he had his share of meltdowns. "Did they really make him leave the school?"

"No, but Cameron was pretty upset about the whole thing. We all were. It took a while for him to get over it, and it was close to the end of the year anyway, so he never ended up going back to Birch Park. He's at Westside now." Byron looked down at his hands, clenched on the table.

"It must be tough for you," said Lauren's mom, setting a bowl of ice cream in front of Byron and another at Will's place. "It's not easy having a child with special needs in the family. Every day is a challenge." She looked over at Lauren. "And sometimes the biggest challenges are for the siblings." She paused. "As parents, it's something we often forget."

Byron wiped his hand across his face. "Thanks, Mrs. Scanlon," he said.

"Ice cream!" said Will. One of his hands hit the bowl in front of him. It went flying and smashed on the floor.

Lauren and Callie burst into giggles, and after a split second Byron and Blake joined in.

"You know what?" said Callie to Lauren as they sat devouring their ice cream a few minutes later. "I think I've got a better idea for our play."

"What is it?" said Lauren.

Callie's gaze wandered around the table to Blake, Will, Byron and, finally, back to Lauren. "I'll tell you later," she said. "But I think you're going to like it."

Chapter Fifteen

Lauren stood in the wings, peering through the curtain at the audience. Her mom and dad were sitting three rows from the front, chatting to Callie's parents and Byron's mom. They'd wanted to sit in the front row, but Lauren and Callie had forbidden it. They didn't want to see those eager faces staring at them from just a few feet away.

Lauren ducked back behind the curtain. Her stomach was all aflutter. She didn't have a huge part, but performing always made her nervous, and she'd never done any acting before.

"I think I'm going to throw up," said Callie from behind her.

Callie was wearing one of Lauren's old dance costumes, a ballet leotard with a long, flowing skirt and a tiara. Her hair was pulled back into a tight bun. With her stage makeup on, she really looked like a prima ballerina.

"You'll be fine," said Lauren. "You were absolutely awesome at rehearsal yesterday."

"Yeah, well, no one was watching then, were they?" Callie glanced at the soccer uniform Lauren was wearing. "I wish I was wearing what you're wearing."

"What are you talking about?" said Lauren. "You look fantastic."

But under her makeup, Callie's face was almost white. Lauren wondered if she really would be sick.

"You'll be fine," she said, crossing her fingers behind her back.

Just then Mr. Pittman stepped onto the stage.

"Here we go," whispered Byron, coming up behind them. "Break a leg."

"It means good luck," Lauren said when she saw Callie staring at him in horror.

Mr. Pittman introduced them and then left the stage.

"You're on," said Lauren to Callie.

Callie took a deep breath. She blew it out and then stepped forward. She strode to center stage and took her position.

"Look at me," she said, throwing her arms wide. "This is what happens when you try to do what other people want you to do." Her voice rang through the auditorium, loud and clear.

A tingle slid up Lauren's spine. Callie was so great!

"I'm a tomboy. Always have been and always will be, and I'm not ashamed to admit it. Not now anyway. But there was a time when I tried to be something I wasn't. And that's what landed me in this ridiculous outfit"—Callie fluffed the skirt out to demonstrate—"and led to the most embarrassing moment of my life.

"My parents always wanted a girl. Not just any girl, but a girly girl. So when I came along, after three boys, they thought their prayers had been answered."

Out of the corner of her eye, Lauren thought she saw Bernice and Gareth exchange surprised glances.

"They dressed me up in skirts," Callie continued, "tied my hair up with fancy ribbons and, of course, enrolled me in dance classes. But no matter how hard I tried to be quiet and dainty and graceful, it just felt wrong. I wanted to wrestle with my brothers, race around on the playground and splash in puddles. I tried to be what they wanted me to be, but I couldn't. And in the end, it took a little boy with a big heart to show me that I needed to be myself and follow my own dreams. When everyone told him he couldn't do something, he didn't listen to them. He went ahead and did it anyway. This is what happened."

Lauren almost cheered out loud. The opening speech was the heart of the play, and Callie had delivered it to perfection. Lauren was so happy she almost forgot to go on. Luckily Byron grabbed her arm as he went past, and she quickly followed him onstage.

She thought she'd be nervous, but she didn't have time for stage fright. The lines seemed to bounce off each other. Before she knew it the curtain had closed on the last act. The applause was deafening. Lauren and Callie threw their arms around each other. It had been the best, and scariest, half hour of their lives. Lauren was sorry it was over.

The curtain rose, and the performers linked arms and took a bow. Then they parted in the middle to allow Miss Chatwal to push Will's wheelchair to the front of the stage. The audience rose in a standing ovation. Lauren whooped and cheered along with the parents. Then she joined arms with Callie again, and they took another bow.

From: scanlon@megamail.com
To: blmalone@bigwater.com

Hi Kat,
I can't believe you're really coming to visit. We're going to have so much fun.

There's tons of things to do here. We can go skating and to the movies and bowling and to the Aquarium or Science World too if you want. I can't wait for you to meet Callie. She's awesome. And guess what? Remember that play we wrote? The one we called BREAKING OUT? Well, Mr. Pittman and Mrs. Dupont chose it for the special assembly! We performed it last week. I was so nervous. Callie was awesome, and Will even had a little part even though he's not in our class. Do you know what he did? He walked, Kat, on his own, in front of the whole school and all the parents and grandparents. He had to walk two steps and then kick the soccer ball into the audience. He practiced so hard for it. I didn't think he'd be able to get it right, but he did. He was awesome. Of course, then he got so excited, he fell over, and everybody laughed, but that's Will for you. He was laughing harder than anyone.

> *Can't wait to see you!*
> *Lauren*

Acknowledgments

It was over twenty years ago that I met the family who provided the inspiration for this book, at a mothers' group following the birth of my first child. We shared play dates, attended birthday parties, drank coffee and swapped stories, and celebrated the birth of our subsequent children. Then our kids hit school age, life got busy, and we lost touch.

I've thought of them many times over the years, and it was during one of these times that Lauren and Will's story came to be. The story is fiction. I've drawn on my experience as a speech pathologist, a writer and a mother in developing it. But I'd like to thank them for the seed of an idea that grew to be this book.

I'd like to thank my sister, Stephanie Dand, for providing early feedback on the story and especially for her insight into schools in British Columbia, as I haven't lived there in many years.

Thank you also to my editor, Tanya Trafford, and the other wonderful people at Orca Book Publishers for their tireless work and continued faith in my writing.

And lastly, thank you to my family, for always supporting me and putting up with the roller coaster of emotions that comes with being a writer.

Sonya Spreen Bates is a Canadian writer living in South Australia. She has written several books for children and adults and has been published in Australia and New Zealand as well as in Canada. She is also trained as a speech-language pathologist and works with children who have communication difficulties.